Out of this World

GOLD TEAM

HELMSDALE PRIMARY
SUTHERLAND

Contents

by Sally Odgers
illustrated by Matt Lin

SCHOLASTIC

S P A C E   S P O R T S

Reading Manga: What is it?

The Japanese word 'manga' has been used for nearly 200 years. It means whimsical pictures (man = whimsical, ga = pictures).

Today, manga is a label for Japanese-style graphic novels, comic books and animated movies (also called anime). What's the difference between a graphic novel and a comic book? The answer is in your hands. Graphic novels are usually quality productions, some-times run to hundreds of pages, and often cover serious subjects. Many Japanese manga focus on topics like the environment, the law, science, history – you name it.

Manga don't all look exactly the same, but they have some things in common:

Big Eyes

Oversized
Expressions

Fast Action

Reading Manga: How to Follow

Each page of a graphic novel is divided into boxes called panels. You follow the panels from left to right and top to bottom, like this:

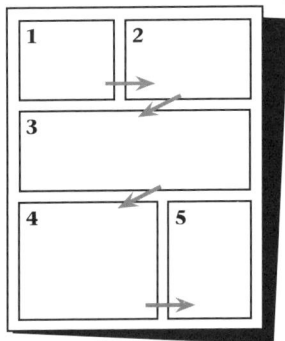

Each panel is like a paragraph in a regular book. It shows you where the characters are, and what they are doing, saying and thinking.

Some panels include a little box at the top (or the bottom), giving you information about what's going on. These are called captions.

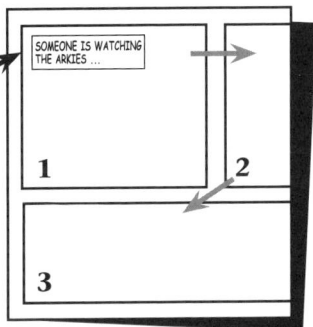

SOMEONE IS WATCHING THE ARKIES ...

DID YOU KNOW?

Traditional Japanese manga look a little different. That's because in Japan, people read from right to left. Japanese manga is read like this:

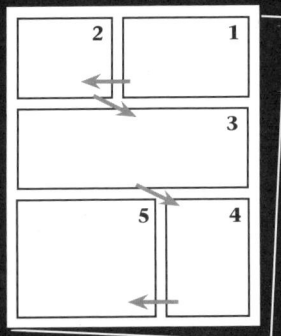

It's easier than it looks!

Reading Manga: Who's talking?

Speech balloons tell you who is speaking, what they're saying, and how.

THIS IS A SPEECH BALLOON.

PSST. I'M WHISPERING. CAN YOU TELL?

THIS IS HOW I SHOUT!

NOW I'M THINKING.

Sometimes the lettering changes, to tell you which words are most important. These words might appear in **BOLD** or LARGE TYPE or in *ITALICS*.

Sometimes a punctuation point is enough to explain what's going on.

!

And how would you show an alien language? Maybe like this:

Reading Manga:
What's that sound?

When you read speech bubbles, you hear manga characters' voices inside your head. There's a way to hear the background noises too – the rumble of thunder, the ringing of a telephone, the crack of a stick underfoot.

Manga artists represent sound effects (or SFX) by placing words over the panels, using lettering to suit each particular sound. It looks like this:

Scary sound

Mechanical sound

Quiet sound

DID YOU KNOW?

Japanese manga SFX are very precise. For example, *bicha bicha* means small splash, *bashan* is a medium splash, and *zaban* is a very big splash. There's even an SFX for total silence: *shiin*.

SFX are used to show emotions as well. The word *unzori* placed next to a character tells you they're feeling bored. If it was *moji moji* they'd be feeling shy, and *shobo shobo* indicates sadness.

Reading Manga:

What's that look on your face?

Manga characters have exaggerated expressions, to help you understand what they're feeling. The first feature everyone notices is the eyes, which may be wide open in:

Shock

Fear

Hope

Closed eyes can mean:

Laughter

Sadness

Noses and chins are more difficult to spot (some characters have no nose at all). This reflects the Japanese preference for delicate features. In manga, big noses and chins are kept for the bad guys.

Reading Manga:

What's that look on your face?

Just like manga characters' eyes, manga mouths are either huge or tiny. A big, wide-open mouth indicates:

Fear

Anger

Happiness

A character with a little mouth may be feeling:

Sad

Thoughtful

Shy

You can also tell a lot about manga characters from the crazy colour or style of their hair. For example, blue hair can mean the character is cool-headed, while orange hair equals determination (and sometimes a fiery temper). Wild, spiky hairstyles show the character is adventurous.

Three kinds of people live on Space Station Nova.

The Stationborn have been there for generations.

Prof

Nonny

Jek

Zita

The Shipborn were born on giant spaceships that wander the Galaxy.

Klikwitz

Mayor Gahdian

The Earthborn came to Nova from Earth.

There has always been rivalry between the three sets of Stationers. But one thing might bring them together: the game they call 3D.

ON SPACE STATION NOVA, 3D BLUE TEAM ARE STARS.

MOST PEOPLE DON'T KNOW THAT PROF, JEK AND ZITA TRAIN SECRETLY AT NIGHT.

THEY HOPE TO FORM THE FIRST 3D JUNIOR TEAM ON NOVA. BUT THE MAYOR'S NEW RULES ARE CAUSING PROBLEMS.

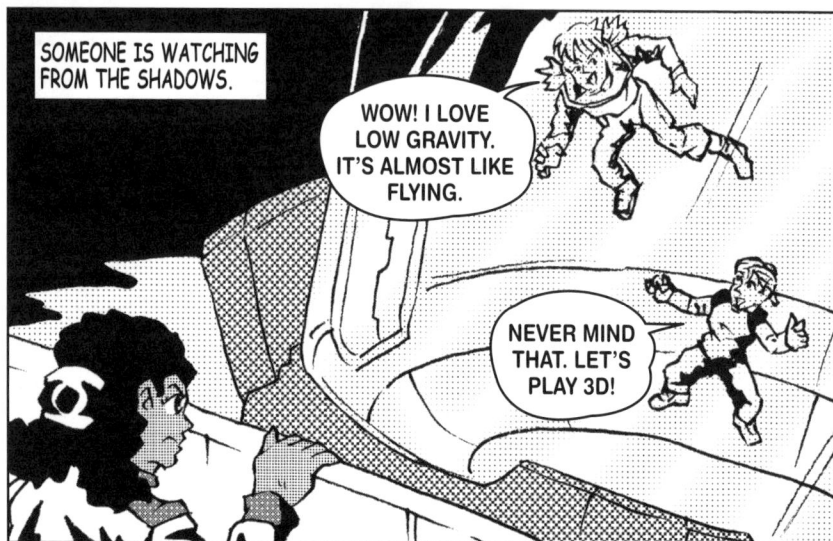

I WISH I COULD PLAY, BUT THEY WOULDN'T HAVE ME. I'M NOT ONE OF THEM.

MEANWHILE, THE MAYOR'S NEPHEW, KLIKWITZ, IS SPYING.

I KNEW THAT NEW GIRL WAS SNEAKING ABOUT LAST NIGHT. SHE MUST BE PLOTTING WITH THOSE OTHER KIDS.

I'M GONNA TELL UNCLE.

PROF, ZITA AND JEK ARE PLEASED WITH THEIR PRACTICE GAME.

OK, YOU GUYS. WE'LL MEET BACK HERE TOMORROW NIGHT.

SURE. I'LL USE THE GRAVITY-CHUTE ON LEVEL THREE BEFORE I COME.

GRAVITY-CHUTE? I MIGHT TRY THAT.

GOODNIGHT, JEK, PROF.

I BET THEY THINK THEY'RE THE ONLY ONES TO THINK OF PLAYING HERE AT NIGHT.

IN THE MORNING, KLIKWITZ VISITS HIS UNCLE TO TELL TALES.

UNCLE, YOU ASKED ME TO WATCH THAT NEW GIRL—

DID I?

I FOUND HER SNEAKING ABOUT AFTER LIGHTS-OUT. AND I FOUND OUT SOMETHING VERY INTERESTING ...

SHE'S NOT THE ONLY ONE SNEAKING ABOUT. SOME KIDS ARE TRESPASSING IN THE 3D DOME!

GOOD WORK, KLIKWITZ! I'LL HAVE MY ASSISTANT LOOK INTO IT.

MAYOR GAHDIAN CALLS IN HIS ASSISTANT, DOC, WHO PLAYS WITH THE 3D BLUE TEAM. HE IS ALSO PROF'S DAD.

SOMEONE IS SNOOPING AROUND THE 3D DOME AT NIGHT, USING UNNECESSARY LIGHT AND GRAV-POWER.

STOP THEM!
THAT NIGHT ...
MAYOR GAHDIAN EXPECTS ME TO WORK ALL DAY AND HALF THE NIGHT AND TRAIN WITH BLUE TEAM?
DOC IS SURPRISED TO MEET A STRANGE GIRL NEAR THE DOME.
HAVE YOU COME TO SEE THE GAME?
WHAT GAME? ARE YOU THE PERSON WHO'S BEEN MESSING ABOUT WITH THE 3D DOME?
NO, I JUST WATCH. YOU'RE THE BLUE TEAM ATTACK PLAYER, RIGHT?
YES. DO I KNOW YOU?

THERE! SEE THAT SPEAR-LEAP? HE'S GREAT WHEN HE CONCENTRATES!

YES ... THEY ALL ARE.

THAT'S IT FOR TONIGHT. ZITA, YOU NEED TO— DAD?

WHAT ARE YOU DOING HERE, DOC?

I COULD ASK YOU LOT THE SAME THING! THE MAYOR IS ANGRY WITH YOU.

WHY DIDN'T YOU TELL ME YOU WERE TRAINING WITH ZITA AND JEK?

YOU DIDN'T HAVE TIME TO TRAIN US, REMEMBER?

BUT DID YOU HAVE TO SNEAK AROUND BEHIND MY BACK?

IT'S NOT YOUR BACK WE WENT BEHIND. IT'S MAYOR GAHDIAN'S.

WELL, HE KNOWS NOW, AND HE'S ORDERED ME TO STOP YOU.

PROF NOTICES A STRANGER.

WHO ARE YOU? ONE OF MAYOR GAHDIAN'S SPIES?

PROF!

I'M NONNY. MY PARENTS GOT WORK ON A SATELLITE, SO I CAME TO LIVE WITH MY GRAN.

SORRY. I MEAN ... I THOUGHT ...

YOU THINK TOO MUCH, PROF.

WELCOME TO NOVA, NONNY.

chapter 2 : A Great Team

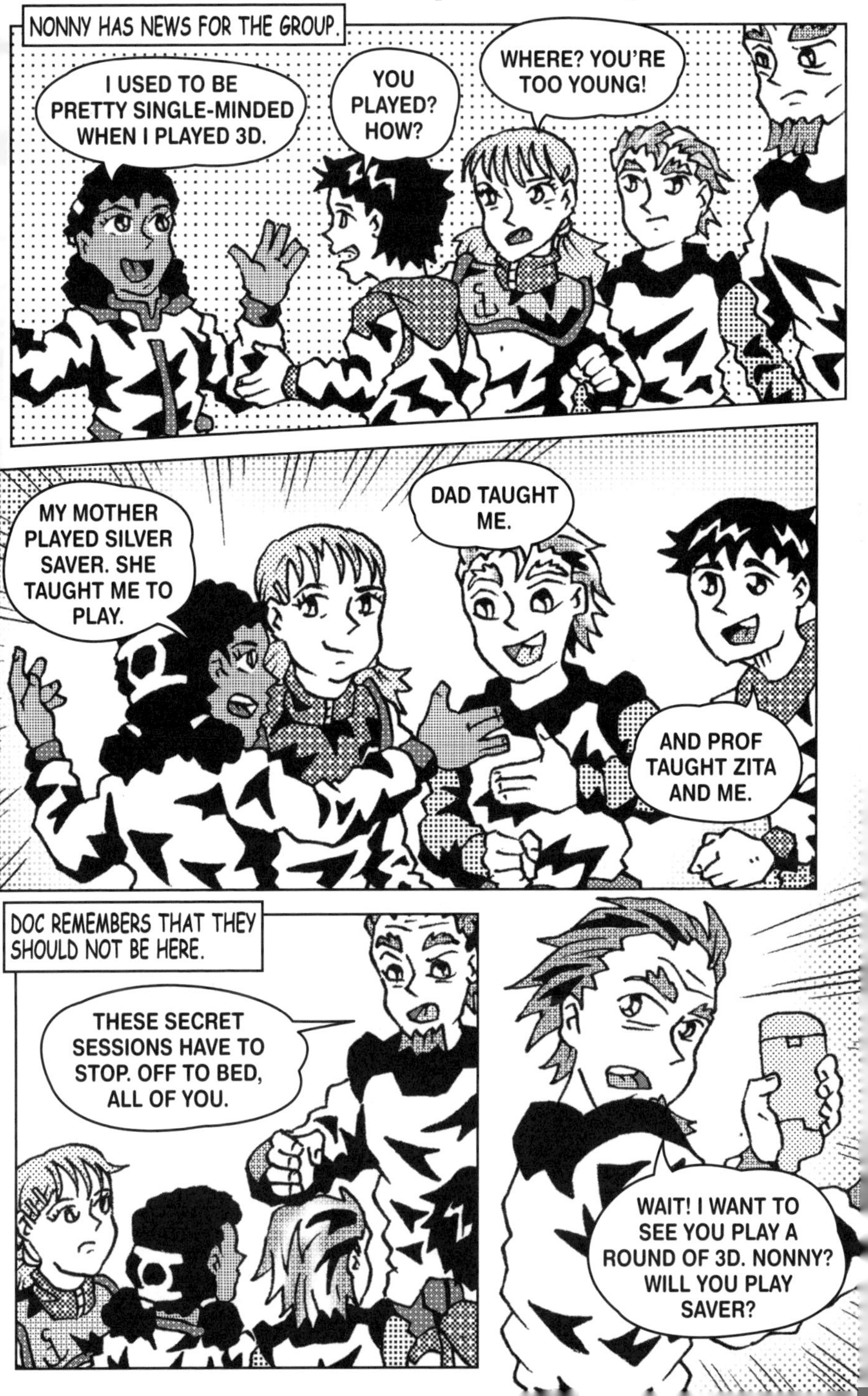

MAYOR GAHDIAN MAKES AN ANNOUNCEMENT.
BLUE TEAM NOVA WILL PLAY THE PENTA PURPLE CHAMPIONS IN A GRAND CHAMPIONSHIP!
THE GRAND PRIZE IS A TEAM SPACE SHUTTLE! THE LOSING TEAM WILL PAY FOR IT!
???!!!
YAY!
THIS IS NEWS TO THE BLUE TEAM.
BUT WE HAVEN'T PRACTISED IN DAYS—
THE MAYOR HAS GOT TO SEE REASON. WE NEED TIME TO TRAIN.
DOC IS ALWAYS TOO BUSY.
SORRY GUYS.
ALL READY TO WIN THIS GAME FOR NOVA, PEOPLE?
THE BLUE TEAM HAS HAD ENOUGH.
WE WON'T WIN, MAYOR GAHDIAN.
BECAUSE WE WON'T PLAY.
WE ARE NOT GOING TO PAY FOR A SHUTTLE. WHY SHOULD WE?

DOC GIVES THE GOOD NEWS TO PROF AND HIS FRIENDS.
I CAN COACH YOU AFTER THE GAME ...
THIS WILL BE GREAT!
YOU MEAN, ME TOO?
OF COURSE, NONNY. YOU'RE VERY GOOD ALREADY.
WATCH OUT, BLUE TEAM ... WE'RE GONNA BE THE BEST!
I WANT TO JOIN YOUR TEAM.
I'M AFRAID THAT WOULD BE—
NO WAY! NOT GOING TO HAPPEN!

YOU'RE ALL AGAINST ME BECAUSE I'M EARTHBORN!

KLIKWITZ, THESE KIDS HAVE ALREADY TRAINED AT 3D. I HAVE TIME TO COACH THEM, BUT NOT TO TEACH YOU AS WELL.

WE DON'T LIKE HIM BECAUSE HE'S A NASTY LITTLE SPY.

I'M GONNA TELL UNCLE YOU'RE MEAN.

I'LL SHOW THEM!

KLIKWITZ COMPLAINS TO MAYOR GAHDIAN.

UNCLE, MAKE DOC PUT ME IN THE JUNIOR TEAM.

LATER, KLIKWITZ, LATER.

THEY CAN'T TREAT ME LIKE THAT. I'LL SHOW THEM ALL!

BLUE TEAM TRAINS HARD FOR THE BIG GAME.
SEE THAT DEFLECT AND ROLL?
GREAT, BLUE TEAM!
I COULD DO THAT.
PROF'S TEAM TRAINS HARD TOO.
THOSE KIDS ARE A CREDIT TO YOU, DOC.
THEY STARTED OFF THEMSELVES.
ANYONE CAN DO THAT IN LOW GRAVITY.
HAVE YOU EVER PLAYED 3D, UNCLE?
OF COURSE NOT. I HATE LOW GRAVITY. IT MAKES ME DIZZY.
KLIKWITZ PLANS A LITTLE EXPERIMENT.
I'M GONNA PRACTISE IN THE GRAVITY-CHUTE ... THEY'LL BE SO MAD WHEN THEY SEE HOW GOOD I AM.
WHAT'S HE UP TO?

- 24 -

MAYOR GAHDIAN IS NOT PLEASED WITH KLIKWITZ.

WHAT'S THIS I HEAR ABOUT YOU PLAYING IN THE GRAVITY-CHUTE?

I NEVER. I DIDN'T. WHO TOLD YOU?

ATTENTION, EVERYONE. SPACE STATION NOVA WELCOMES THE PENTA PURPLE CHAMPIONS!

I'LL DEAL WITH YOU LATER. I HAVE TO GO AND OVERSEE THE GAME.

I HAD TO JUMP INTO THE GRAVITY-CHUTE. SOMEONE HAD SABOTAGED IT. COME AND SEE!

KLIKWITZ GETS HIS UNCLE TO LOOK DOWN THE GRAVITY-CHUTE ON THE WAY TO THE GAME.

I CAN'T SEE ANYTHING.

LOOK OUT, UNCLE!

PROF'S GOING TO – NO! STOP! LEAVE MY UNCLE ALONE!

ARGHHHH!

KLIKWITZ HURRIES TO THE 3D DOME.

NOW UNCLE'S OUT OF THE WAY ...

I'M GONNA TELL EVERYONE HOW MEAN DOC IS!

Panel 1: KLIKWITZ HAS A PLAN ...

EVERYONE GATHER AT THE 3D DOME TO WATCH BLUE TEAM NOVA PLAY THE PENTA PURPLE CHAMPIONS.

I'M GONNA SHOW THEM ALL.

Panel 2: THE PENTA PURPLE CHAMPIONS ARRIVE AT THE DOME.

PLEASE WELCOME OUR VISITING TEAM.

WHERE'S THE MAYOR?

LOOK AT THOSE UNIFORMS.

THEY LOOK GREAT!

Panel 3: BLUE TEAM GETS A BIG WELCOME.

YAYYYYYYYY! BLUE TEAM!

Panel 4: SUDDENLY, JUST AS THE GAME IS ABOUT TO START...

YOU SHOULDN'T CHEER THEM! DOC'S MEAN!

WHO IS THAT?

WHAT'S THAT KID DOING?

KLIKWITZ LOSES HIS BALANCE.
ARGHHHHH! HELLLLLLP!
IS THIS SOME KIND OF JOKE?
IT'S THE MAYOR'S NEPHEW. COME ON, TEAM!
THE NOVA TEAMS LEAP INTO ACTION.
WE'LL GET YOU.
HOLD ON, KLIKWITZ.
JUST AS HELP ARRIVES KLIKWITZ PANICS.
ARGHHHH! YOU'RE HURTING ME!
OAFFFF!
UGHHH.
THACK!
THACK!
KLIKWITZ, BLUE CAPTAIN AND DOC FALL.
UGHHH.
UGHHH.
WAM!

THE PENTA PURPLE CAPTAIN HAS AN OBJECTION.

JUNIOR TEAM? WHAT'S THAT? AND THIS ONE IS SHIPBORN!

THAT'S AGAINST THE RULES!

NOT FOR A JUNIOR TEAM. AND ONE DAY ALL 3D TEAMS WILL REPRESENT ALL THE PEOPLES!

ALL RIGHT. LET'S GET THIS FARCE OVER.

RIGHT, TEAM, LET'S PLAY 3D!

THE GAME BETWEEN PENTA PURPLE CHAMPIONS AND GOLD TEAM JUNIOR MAKES HISTORY!

GOAL TO GOLD TEAM JUNIOR.

YAY GOLD TEAM JUNIOR! WHAT A TEAM!

THIS WAS ALL MY IDEA. DOC, YOU HAVE A NEW JOB. YOU WILL COACH THIS TEAM!

WHAT ABOUT BLUE TEAM?

IT'LL BE A WHILE BEFORE WE CAN PLAY AGAIN.

Gold Team
Nova Speak

3D A skilled ball game played on space stations.

Deflect and Roll A move made by 3D players.

Dome A low-gravity cylinder with see-through walls, where 3D is played.

Earthborn People born on Earth.

Gravity-chute A cylinder in which gravity can be changed.

Grav-power Power used to change gravity in the 3D dome.

Holoplayers Holographic 3D players, used to train teams.

Spear-leap A move made by 3D players.

Shipborn People born on huge spaceships.

Stationborn People born on big space stations, like *Nova*.

GOLD TEAM JUNIOR WINS ITS VERY FIRST GAME.
GOLD TEAM JUNIOR WINS BY A SLIM MARGIN FROM PENTA PURPLE CHAMPIONS.
I GUESS THIS MEANS WE GET A BRAND-NEW SHUTTLE?
I'M SO GONNA GET EVEN WITH PROF ONE DAY.

INTRODUCING GOLD TEAM JUNIOR!
JEK NOVA, GOLD DEFENCE.
NONNY OCTAVIAN, GOLD SAVER.
PROF NOVA, GOLD CAPTAIN.
AND ZITA TARANTELLA ... GOLD ATTACK!